Lz
childrey
38

The Stars in the Sky

and other magical stories

Compiled by Vic Parker

Miles Kelly

First published in 2012 by Miles Kelly Publishing Ltd
Harding's Barn, Bardfield End Green, Thaxted, Essex, CM6 3PX, UK

2 4 6 8 10 9 7 5 3 1

Publishing Director Belinda Gallagher

Creative Director Jo Cowan

Editorial Director Rosie McGuire

Editor Carly Blake

Senior Designer Joe Jones

Editorial Assistant Lauren White

Production Manager Elizabeth Collins

Reprographics Anthony Cambray, Stephan Davis, Jennifer Hunt

ISBN 978-1-84810-575-1

Printed in China

British Library Cataloguing-in-Publication Data
A catalogue record for this book is available from the British Library

ACKNOWLEDGEMENTS

The publishers would like to thank the following artists who have contributed to this book:
Cover: Lesley Danson at The Bright Agency
Advocate Art: Alida Massari
The Bright Agency: Marcin Piwowarski, Tom Sperling
Marsela Hajdinjak

All other artwork from the Miles Kelly Artwork Bank

The publishers would like to thank the following sources for the use of their photographs:
Shutterstock: (page decorations) Dragana Francuski Tolimir
Dreamstime: (frames) Gordan

Every effort has been made to acknowledge the source and copyright holder of each picture.
Miles Kelly Publishing apologises for any unintentional errors or omissions.

Made with paper from a sustainable forest

www.mileskelly.net info@mileskelly.net

www.factsforprojects.com

Contents

The Stone-cutter

From Andrew Lang's *Crimson Fairy Book*

ONCE UPON A TIME there lived a stone-cutter, who went every day to a great rock in the side of a big mountain and cut out slabs. He understood very well the kinds of stones wanted for different purposes, and as he was a careful workman he had plenty of customers. For a long time he was quite contented, and asked for nothing better than what he had.

The Stone-cutter

Now in the mountain dwelled a spirit which now and then appeared to men and granted wishes. The stone-cutter, however, had never seen this spirit, and only shook his head, with an unbelieving air, when anyone spoke of it. But a time was coming when he would change his opinion.

One day the stone-cutter carried a gravestone to the house of a rich man, and saw there all sorts of beautiful things, of which he had never even dreamed. "Oh, if only I were rich," he sighed, "and could sleep in a bed with silken curtains and golden tassels, how happy I should be!"

And a voice answered him: "Your wish is heard — a rich man you shall be!"

The stone-cutter looked round, but could see nobody. He thought it was all his fancy, and picked up his tools and went home. But when he reached the little house where he lived, he stood still with amazement, for instead of his wooden hut was a stately palace filled with splendid furniture, and most splendid of all was the bed, in every respect like the one he had envied. He was nearly beside himself with joy, and in his new life the old one was soon forgotten.

It was now the beginning of summer, and each day the sun blazed more fiercely. One morning the heat was so great that the stone-cutter could scarcely breathe, and he determined he would stay at home till the evening. It was rather dull, for he had never learned how to amuse himself, and he was peeping through the closed blinds to see what was going on in the street, when a little carriage passed by, drawn by servants dressed in blue and silver. In the carriage sat a prince, and over his head a golden umbrella was held, to protect him from the sun's bright rays.

"Oh, if I were only a prince!" said the stone-cutter to himself, as the carriage vanished round the corner. "Oh, if only I could go in such a carriage and have a golden umbrella held over me, how happy I should be!"

And the voice of the mountain spirit answered: "Your wish is heard — a prince you shall be."

And a prince he was. Before his carriage rode one company of men and another behind it. Servants dressed in scarlet and gold bore him along, the coveted umbrella was held over his head, everything heart could desire was his.

But yet it was not enough.

He looked round still for something to wish for, and when he saw that in spite of the water he poured on his grass the rays of the sun scorched it, and that in spite of the umbrella held over his head each day his face grew browner and browner, he

cried in his anger: "The sun is mightier than I. Oh, if I were only the sun!"

And the mountain spirit answered: "Your wish is heard – the sun you shall be."

And the sun he was, and felt himself proud in his power. He shot his beams above and below, on earth and in heaven. He burned up the grass in the fields and scorched the faces of princes as well as of poorer folk. But in a short time he began to grow tired of his might, for there seemed nothing left for him to do. Discontent once more filled his soul, and when a cloud covered his face, and hid the earth from him, he cried in his anger: "Does the cloud hold captive my rays, and is it mightier than I? Oh, that I were a cloud, and mightier than any!"

And the mountain spirit answered: "Your wish is heard – a cloud you shall be!"

And a cloud he was. He caught the sun's beams and held them, and to his joy the earth grew green again and flowers blossomed. But that was not enough for him, and for days and weeks he poured forth rain till the rivers overflowed their banks, and the crops of rice stood in water. Towns and villages were destroyed, only the great rock on the mountain side remained unmoved. The cloud was amazed and cried out: "Is the rock, then, mightier than I? Oh, if I were only the rock!"

And the mountain spirit answered: "Your wish is heard – the rock you shall be!"

And the rock he was. Proudly he stood, and neither the heat of the sun nor the force of the rain could move him. "This is better than all!" he said to himself. But one day he heard a strange noise at his

feet, and when he looked down to see what it could be, he saw a stone-cutter driving tools into his surface. Even while he looked, a trembling feeling ran all through him, and a great block broke off and fell upon the ground. Then he cried in his wrath: "Is a mere child of earth mightier than a rock? Oh, if I were only a man!"

And the mountain spirit answered: "Your wish is heard. A man once more you shall be!"

And a man he was, and in the sweat of his brow he toiled again at his trade of stone-cutting. His bed was hard and his food scanty, but he had learned to be satisfied with it, and did not long to be something or somebody else. And as he never asked for things he had not got, or desired to be greater and mightier than other people, he was happy at long last, and he heard the voice of the mountain spirit no longer.

A Grand Transformation Scene

An extract from *Vice Versa* by F Anstey

Dick Bultitude is a Victorian schoolboy. The school holidays are at an end, and his father, Paul, is saying goodbye as Dick is about to set off back to boarding school, where he is very unhappy.

MR BULTITUDE selected from the coins before him a florin, two shillings, and two sixpences, which he pushed across to his son, who looked at them with disappointment.

"That's a lot of pocket money for a young fellow like you," Mr Bultitude observed. "Don't buy anything foolish with it, and if, towards the end of the term you want a little more, and write an intelligible letter asking for it, and I think proper to let you have it – why, you'll get it, you know."

Dick had not the courage to ask for more, much as he longed to do so, so he put the money in his purse. There, he seemed to find something which had escaped his memory, for he took out a small parcel and unfolded it.

"I nearly forgot," he said, "I didn't like to take it without asking you, but may I have it?"

"Eh?" said Mr Bultitude, sharply. "What's that? Something else – what is it you want now?"

"It's only that stone Uncle Marmaduke brought Mamma from India – the thing, he said, they called a 'Pagoda stone', or something, out there."

"Pagoda stone? The boy means Garudâ Stone. I should like to know how you got hold of that – you've been meddling in my drawers, now, haven't you? A thing I will not put up with, as I've told you over and over again."

"No," said Dick, "I found it in the drawing-room – but I may have it, mayn't I?" he persisted.

"Have it? You may certainly not. What could you possibly want with a thing like that? Give it to me."

Dick handed it over reluctantly. It was not much to look at, a little square tablet of greyish green stone, pierced at one angle, and having on two of its faces faint traces of mysterious letters or symbols, which time had made very difficult to distinguish.

It looked harmless enough as Mr Bultitude took it – there was no kindly hand to hold him back, no warning voice to hint that there might be sleeping within that small marble block the pent-up energy of long-forgotten Eastern magic, ready to awake at the first words which had power to stir it.

Paul Bultitude put on his glasses to examine the stone more carefully. Then he looked up and said once more, "What use would a thing like this be to you?"

Dick would have considered it a very valuable

prize indeed. He could have shown it to admiring friends under the desk during boring lessons, he could have played with it and invented astonishing legends of its powers, and when he had grown tired of it at last, he could have swapped it for something else. But he could not find either courage or words to explain himself. So he only said awkwardly, "Oh, I don't know, I would just like it."

"Well, any way," said Paul, "you certainly won't have it. It must be worth something, whatever it is, as the only thing your Uncle Marmaduke was ever known to give to anybody."

"Isn't it a talisman, a charm, though?" said Dick.

"I'm sure I can't tell you," yawned Paul, "how do you mean?"

"I don't know, only Uncle Marmaduke once said something about it. Maybe it cures people of things. If you would only let me have it, perhaps I might find out, you know."

"You might," said his father drily, "but you won't

have the chance. If it has a secret, I will find it out for myself… and, by the way, I hear your taxi arriving – at last."

There was a sound of wheels outside, and, as Dick heard them, he grew desperate to ask for something else, something even more important. He got up and moved timidly towards his father.

"Father," he said, "there's something I want to say. Do let me ask you now."

"Well, what is it?" said Paul. "Make haste, you haven't much time."

"It's this. I want you to… to let me leave Grimstone's at the end of the term."

"Let you leave Grimstone's!" said Paul angrily. "What do you mean? It's an excellent school!"

"I'd like to go to Marlborough, or Harrow, or somewhere," whimpered Dick. "My friend Jolland's going to Harrow at Easter. The head, Dr Grimstone, is nice to pupils he likes, but he doesn't like me – he's always blaming me for something – and I hate some of the other boys there. Do let me leave!"

"It's all ridiculous nonsense, I tell you," said Paul angrily. "You will stay at Grimstone's for as long as I say, and there's an end of that!"

At this, Dick began to sob, which was more than his father could bear. To do Paul justice, he had not meant to be quite so harsh, and, a little ashamed, he sought to justify himself by running through all the reasons why Grimstone's was such a good school.

"Now, you know, it's no use to cry like that," he began. "It's the usual thing for boys at school, I'm quite aware, to go about fancying they're very hard done by, and miserable, and all the rest of it! It's one of those things all boys have to go through. And you mark my words, my boy, when they grow up and go out into the world, they look back at school as the happiest time of their life!"

"Well," said Dick, "then I hope it won't be the happiest time in mine! You may have been happy at the school you went to, perhaps, but I don't believe you would very much care about being a boy again like me, and going back to Grimstone's!"

Paul still had the stone in his hand as he replied, smirking, "Perhaps you will believe me, when I tell you that, old as I am, I only wish that I could be a boy again, going back to school, like you."

As he spoke, he felt a shiver, followed by a curious shrinking sensation all over. And the armchair in which he sat seemed to have grown so much bigger all at once. He felt a passing surprise, but decided it must be his imagination, and went on as before.

"I should like it, but what's the good of wishing? I'm an old man and you're a young boy. There's nothing anyone can… What the devil are you giggling about?"

For Dick, after some seconds of half-frightened and open-mouthed staring, had suddenly burst into a fit of sniggering, which he was trying hard to stop.

This naturally annoyed Mr Bultitude, and he went on with immense dignity, "I'm not aware that I've been saying anything particularly ridiculous. You seem to be amused?"

"Don't!" gasped Dick. "It, it isn't anything you're saying… it's, it's… oh, can't you feel any difference?"

"The sooner you go back to school the better!" said Paul angrily. "I've had quite enough of this. Leave the room this instant!"

Dick, however, remained where he was, shaking with laughter, while his father sat stiffly on his chair, and tried to ignore his son's strange behaviour.

At last his patience gave out, and he said coldly, "Now, perhaps, you will be good enough to let me know what the joke is?"

Dick's voice was hoarse with laughter as he spoke.

"Haven't you found out yet? Go and look at yourself in the mirror!"

Mr Bultitude walked to the mirror, wondering whether he had a smudge on his face or something wrong with his collar and tie. But no sooner had Paul met his reflection than he started back in horror – then returned and stared again, and again.

Surely, surely, this could not be he!

He had expected to see his own familiar, portly presence there – but the mirror insisted upon reflecting the figure of his son Dick! The reflection opposite him moved when he moved, returned when he returned, copied his every gesture!

He turned round upon his son in anger. "You've been playing some of your tricks with this mirror," he cried fiercely. "What have you done to it?"

"Done! How could I do anything to it?"

"Then," stammered Paul, "do you mean to tell me you can see any – changes to my appearance? Tell me the truth now!"

"I should think so!" said Dick. "It's very queer, but just look here," and he came over to the mirror and placed himself by the side of his horrified father. "Why," he said, with another giggle, "we're as like as two peas!"

The glass reflected now two small boys, each with chubby cheeks and golden hair, both dressed exactly alike, in Eton jackets and broad white collars. The only difference between them was that, while one face wore an expression of glee and satisfaction, the other – which Mr Bultitude was beginning to fear must belong to him – was drawn with dismay and bewilderment.

"Dick," said Paul faintly, "what is all this? What has happened?"

"I'm sure I don't know, I haven't done anything!" protested Dick. "You

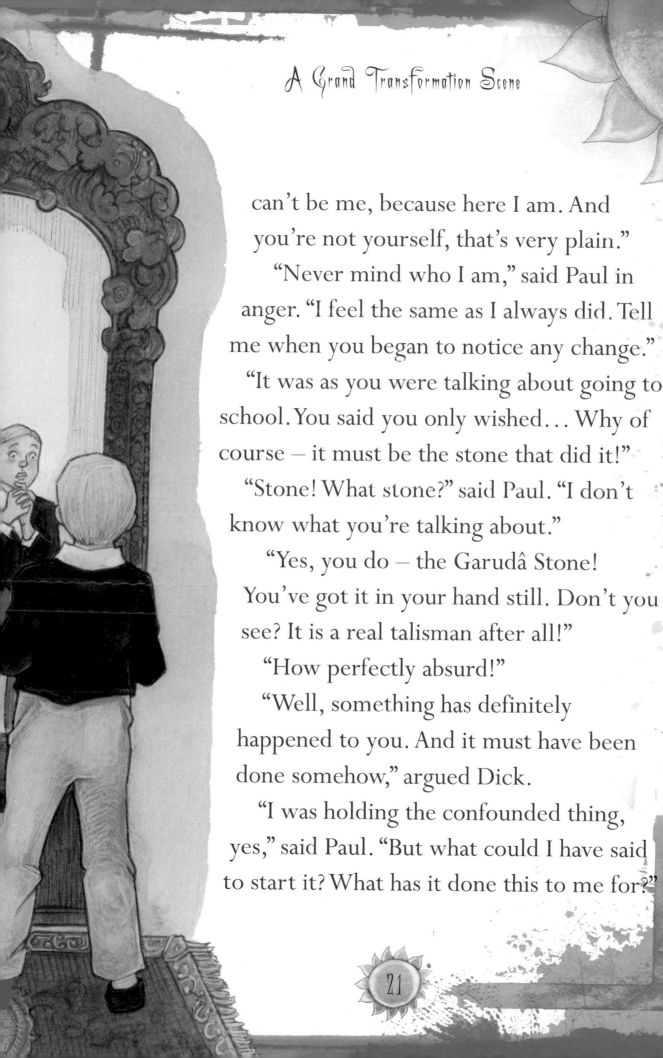

can't be me, because here I am. And you're not yourself, that's very plain."

"Never mind who I am," said Paul in anger. "I feel the same as I always did. Tell me when you began to notice any change."

"It was as you were talking about going to school. You said you only wished… Why of course – it must be the stone that did it!"

"Stone! What stone?" said Paul. "I don't know what you're talking about."

"Yes, you do – the Garudâ Stone! You've got it in your hand still. Don't you see? It is a real talisman after all!"

"How perfectly absurd!"

"Well, something has definitely happened to you. And it must have been done somehow," argued Dick.

"I was holding the confounded thing, yes," said Paul. "But what could I have said to start it? What has it done this to me for?"

"I know!" cried Dick. "Don't you remember? You said you wished you were a boy again, like me."

"Wished!" echoed Mr Bultitude. "I never thought of that," he said, "The thing's a wishing stone! You have to hold it, I suppose, and then say what you wish aloud, and there you are. If that's the case, I can put it all right by simply wishing myself back again."

He took the stone, and got into a corner where he began repeating the words, "I wish I was back again," "I wish I was the man I was five minutes ago," and "I wish all this had not happened". He tried with the stone held in his left hand, as well as his right, sitting and standing, under all the various conditions he could think of, but absolutely nothing came of it.

"I don't like this," he said at last, giving it up with a crestfallen air. "I can't make it work any more!"

"Perhaps," suggested Dick, who still looked gleeful, "perhaps it's one of those talismans that only give you one wish, and you've had it, you know?"

"Then it's all over!" groaned Paul. "What the devil

am I to do? If I don't see my way out of this soon, I shall go raving mad!"

All at once, an idea came to him. He was forced to agree that there must be some magic power in this Garudâ Stone. It was plain too that the talisman would no longer work for him. But perhaps it would grant a wish for someone else? If Dick took the stone and wished that his father would return back to normal, maybe everything would be put right.

Mr Bultitude explained his plan to Dick at once.

"I may as well try," Dick said, with a mischievous sparkle in his eye, "give the stone to me."

"Take it," said Paul, desperately. "Take it, and wish your poor old father himself again!"

Dick took the stone, and held it thoughtfully in his hand for some moments.

"I suppose," he asked, "when you are yourself again, things would go on just as usual?"

"I… I hope so."

"I mean you will go on sitting here, and I shall

go off to Grimstone's?"

"Of course, of course," said Paul, "I'm sure you quite understand what has to be done, so get on. We might be found like this any minute."

"That settles it," said Dick.

"Settles what?" asked Mr Bultitude, struck by something peculiar in the boy's manner.

"Well, I've thought of something fairer. You see, you wished to be a boy just like me. Well, if I wish to be a man just like you were ten minutes ago, that will put things all right again, won't it?"

"Are you mad?" cried Paul, horrified. "Why that would be worse than ever! Give me that stone."

But Dick was too quick for him. Slipping off the table, he planted himself firmly on the hearthrug, with the hand that held the stone clenched behind his back, and the other raised in self-defence.

"I wish I was a man like you were just now!" he cried in triumph.

And as he spoke, Mr Bultitude watched his son

swell into the exact copy of his former self!

The transformed Dick began to skip round the room in glee. "It's all right, you see," he said. "The old stone's as good as ever. You can't say anyone would ever know, to look at us."

And then he threw himself into a chair, and began to laugh excitedly at the success of his brilliant idea.

The Lad Who Went to the North Wind

From *Popular Tales from the Norse*
by Sir George Webbe Dasent

ONCE ON A TIME there was an old widow who had one son, and as she was poorly and weak, her son had to go up into the safe to fetch meal for cooking. But when he got outside the safe, and was just going down the steps, there came the North Wind, puffing and blowing, caught up the meal, and so away with it through the air. Then the lad went back into the safe for more, but when he came out again on the steps, the North Wind came again and carried off the meal with a puff, and, more than that, he did so the third time.

At this the lad got very angry. He determined to look up the North Wind and ask for his meal back. So off he went, but the way was long, and he walked and walked, but at last he came to the North Wind's house.

"Good day!" said the lad. "Thank you for coming to see us yesterday."

"Good day!" answered the North Wind, in a voice that was loud and gruff. "And thanks for coming to see me. What do you want?"

"I only wished to ask you to be so good as to let me have back that meal which you took from me," said the lad, "for we haven't very much to live on, and if you're to go on snapping up the last morsel we have,

27

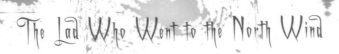

there'll be nothing for it but for us to starve."

"I haven't got your meal," said the North Wind, "but if you are in such need, I'll give you a cloth which will get you everything you wish, if you only say, 'Cloth, spread yourself, and serve up all kind of good dishes!'"

With this the lad was well content.

As the way was so long he couldn't get home in one day, so he turned into an inn on the way, and when they were going to sit down to supper he laid the cloth on a table which stood in the corner, and said, "Cloth, spread yourself, and serve up all kinds

of good dishes." He had scarce said so before the cloth did as it was bid, and all who stood by thought it a fine thing, but most of all the landlady. So, when all were fast asleep at the dead of night, she took the lad's cloth, and put another in its stead, just like the one he had got from the North Wind, but which couldn't so much as serve up a bit of dry bread.

When the lad woke, he took his cloth and went off with it, and that day he got home to his mother. "Now," said he, "I've been to the North Wind's house, and a good fellow he is, for he gave me this cloth, and when I only say to it, 'Cloth, spread yourself, and serve up all kinds of good dishes,' I get any sort of food I please."

"All very true, I daresay," said his mother, "but seeing is believing, and I shan't believe it till I see it for myself."

So the lad made haste, drew out a table, laid the cloth on it, and said: "Cloth, spread yourself, and serve up all kinds of good dishes."

But not even a piece of dry bread did the cloth serve up.

"Well," said the lad, "there's no help for it but to go to the North Wind again," and away he went.

Late in the afternoon, he came to where the North Wind lived.

"Good evening!" said the lad.

"Good evening!" said the North Wind.

"I want my rights for that meal of ours which you took," said the lad, "for, as for that cloth I got, it isn't worth a penny."

"I've got no meal," said the North Wind, "but yonder you have a ram which coins nothing but golden ducats as soon as you wish: 'Ram, ram! Make money!'"

So the lad thought this a fine thing.

It was too far to get home that day, so he turned in for the night to the same inn where he had slept before. Before he called for anything, he tried the truth of what the North Wind had said of the ram, and found it all right, but, when the landlord saw that, he thought it was a famous ram, and, when the lad had fallen asleep, he took another which couldn't coin gold ducats, and changed the two.

Next morning off went the lad, and when he got home to his mother, he said: "After all, the North Wind is a jolly fellow, for he has given me a ram which can coin golden ducats if I only say 'Ram, ram! Make money!'"

"All very true, I daresay," said his mother, "but I shan't believe any such stuff until I see the ducats made for myself."

"Ram, ram! Make money!" said the lad, but if the ram made anything, it wasn't money.

So the lad went back again to the North Wind, and blew him up, and said the ram was worth nothing, and he must have his rights for the meal.

"Well!" said the North Wind. "I've nothing else to give you, except for that old stick in the corner yonder, but it is a stick of that kind that if you wish:

'Stick, stick! Lay on!' it lays on till you say: 'Stick, stick! Now stop!'"

As the way was long, the lad turned in this night too to the landlord, but as he could pretty well guess how things stood as to the cloth and the ram, he lay down at once on the bench and began to snore, as if he were asleep.

Now the landlord, who easily saw that the stick must be worth something, hunted up one which was like it, and when he heard the lad snore, was going to change the two. But, just as the landlord was about to take it, the lad bawled out: "Stick, stick! Lay on!"

So the stick began to beat the landlord, till he jumped over chairs, and tables, and benches, and yelled and roared: "Oh my!

32

Oh my! Bid the stick be still, else it will beat me to death, and you shall have back both your cloth and your ram."

When the lad thought the landlord had got enough, he said: "Stick, stick! Now stop!"

Then he took the cloth and put it into his pocket, and went home with his stick in his hand, leading the ram by a cord round its horns.

And so he got his rights for the meal he had lost.

The Stars in the Sky

From *More English Fairy Tales* by Joseph Jacobs

ONCE UPON A TIME there was a lassie who wept all day to have the stars in the sky to play with. She wouldn't have this, and she wouldn't have that, but it was always the stars she would have. So one day, off she went to find them. And she walked and walked, till by and by she came to a mill-dam.

"Goode'en to ye," says she, "I'm seeking the stars in the sky to play with. Have you seen any?"

"Oh, yes," said the mill-dam. "They shine in my face o' nights till I can't sleep for them. Jump in and perhaps you'll find one."

So she jumped in, and swam about and swam about, but ne'er a one could she see. So she went on till she came to a brooklet.

"Goode'en to ye, Brooklet," says she. "I'm seeking the stars in the sky to play with. Have you seen any?"

"Yes, indeed," said the Brooklet. "They glint on my banks at night. Paddle about and maybe you'll find one."

So she paddled and paddled, but ne'er a one did she find. So on she went till she came to the Good Folk.

"Goode'en to ye, Good Folk," says she. "I'm looking for the stars in the sky to play with. Have ye seen e'er a one?"

"Why, yes," said the Good Folk. "They shine on the grass here o' night. Dance with us and maybe you'll find one."

And she danced and danced, but ne'er a one did she see. So down she sat and wept.

"Oh dearie me," says she, "I've swam and I've

paddled and I've danced, and if ye'll not help me I shall never find the stars in the sky to play with."

But the Good Folk whispered together, and one of them took her by the hand and said, "Go forward – and mind you take the right road. Ask Four Feet to carry you to No Feet at all, and tell No Feet at all to carry you to the stairs without steps, and if you can climb that…"

"Oh, shall I be among the stars in the sky then?" cried the lassie.

"If you'll not be, then you'll be elsewhere," said the Good Folk, and set to dancing again.

So on she went again with a light heart, and by and by she came to a saddled horse, tied to a tree.

"Goode'en to ye, Beast," said she. "I'm seeking the stars in the sky to play with. Will you give me a lift, for all my bones are an-aching."

"Nay," said the horse, "I know naught of the stars in the sky, and I'm here to do the bidding of the Good Folk, not my own will."

"Well," said she, "it's from the Good Folk I come, and they bade me tell Four Feet to carry me to No Feet at all."

"That's another story," said he, "jump up and ride with me."

So they rode and rode, till they got out of the forest and found themselves at the edge of the sea. And on the water was a wide glistening path running straight out towards a beautiful thing that rose out of the water and went up into the sky, and was all the colours in the world, blue and red and green, and wonderful to look at.

"Now get you down," said the horse. "I've brought ye to the end of the land, and that's as much as Four Feet can do."

"But," said the lassie, "where's No Feet at all, and where's the stair without steps?"

"I know not," said the horse. "Goode'en to ye." And off he went.

The lassie stood and looked at the water, till a

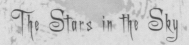

strange kind of fish came swimming up to her feet.

"Goode'en to ye, big fish," says she. "I'm looking for the stars in the sky, and for the stairs that climb up to them. Will ye show me the way?"

"Nay," said the fish, "I can't unless you bring me word from the Good Folk."

"Yes, indeed," said she. "They said Four Feet would bring me to No Feet at all, and No Feet at all would carry me to the stairs without steps."

"Ah, well," said the fish, "that's all right then. Get on my back and hold fast."

And off he went — *kerplash!* — into the water, along the silver path, towards the bright arch. And the nearer they came, the brighter the sheen of it, till she had to shade her eyes.

And as they came to the foot of it, she saw it was a broad bright road, sloping up and away into the sky, and at the far, far end of it she could see wee shining things dancing about.

"Now," said the fish, "here you are, and yon's the stair. Climb up, if you can, but hold on fast." And off he splashed through the water.

So she climbed and climbed, but ne'er a step higher did she get. The light was before her and around her, and the water behind her, and the more she struggled the more she was forced down into the dark and the cold, and the more she climbed, the deeper she fell.

But she climbed and climbed, till she got dizzy in the light and shivered with the cold, and dazed with fear – and she let clean go, and sank down… down… down…

And – *bang!* – she landed on hard boards, and found herself sitting, weeping and wailing, by the bedside at home all alone.